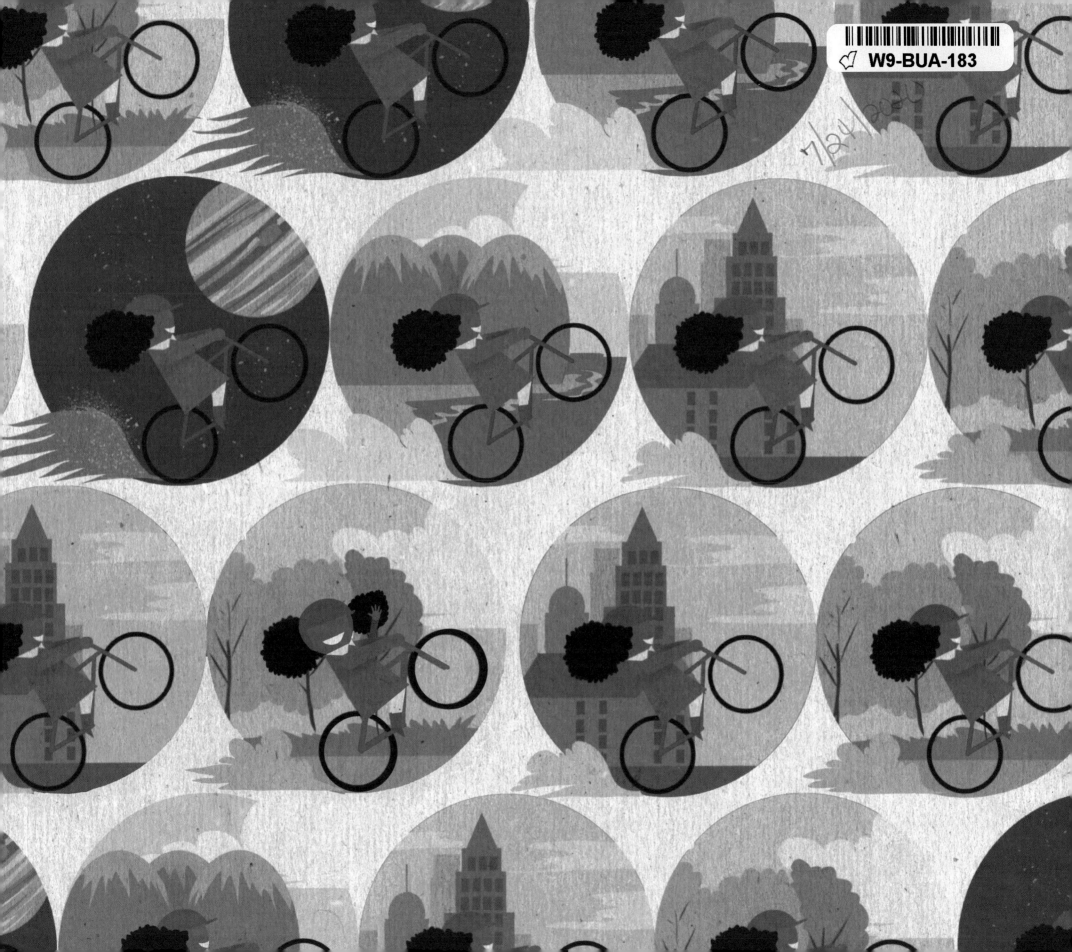

Fast Enough

BESSIE STRINGFIELD'S FIRST RIDE

JOEL CHRISTIAN GILL

Have you ever been told you are not enough?

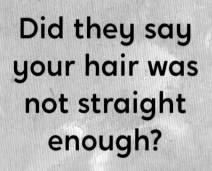

Did they say
your hair was
not straight
enough?

Did they say
your belly
was not flat
enough?

Bessie was told that she was not enough.

But the boys yelled . . .

They zoomed away.

Bessie's not fast enough.

Later that night, she prayed for Mama and prayed for her toys, then said, "Mama said to ask if girls are supposed to ride bikes."

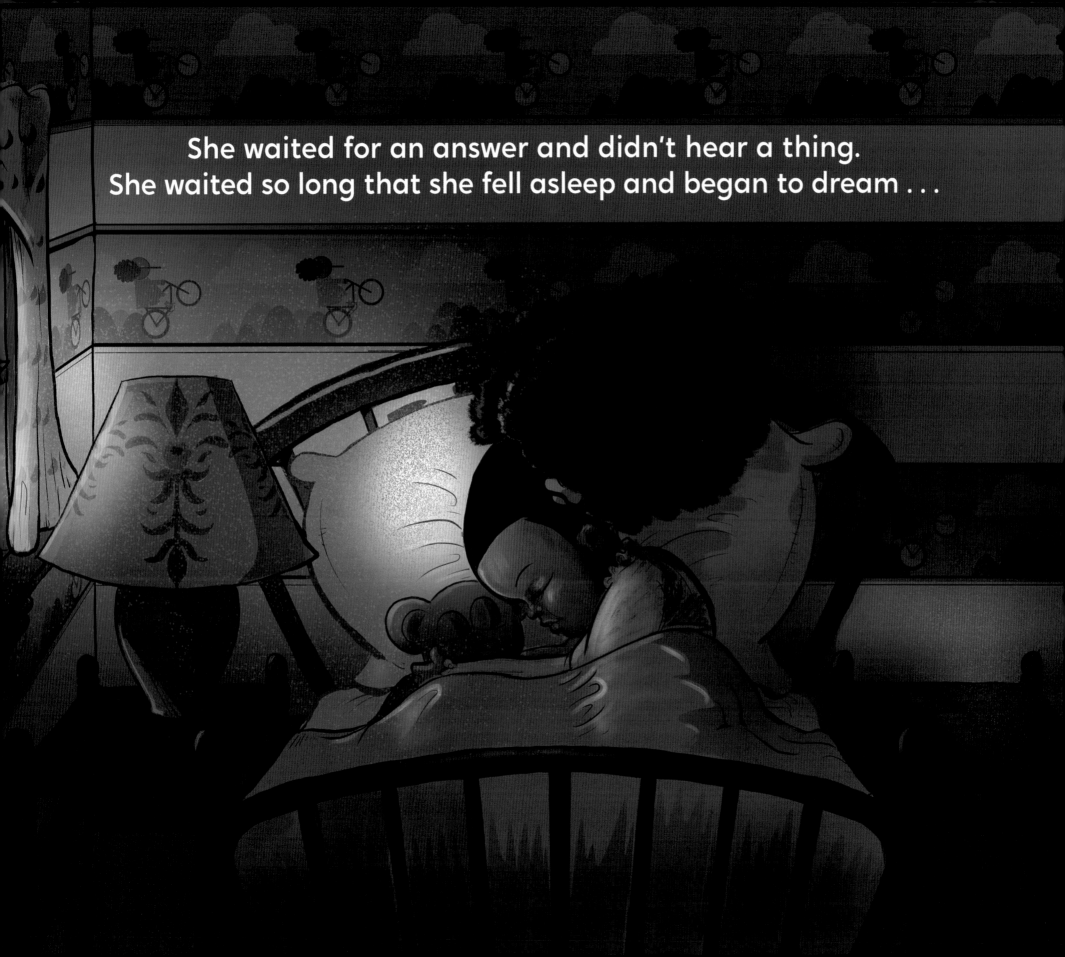

She rode up hills and down hills,
through valleys and by oceans.

She rode so fast she even raced over the water!

She rode through cities and between tall buildings.

She rode so fast she even raced
up into the night sky.

When Bessie woke up, she knew just what to do.

The very next afternoon, the boys got ready for their afternoon race, laughing as they rode up.

Bessie waited.

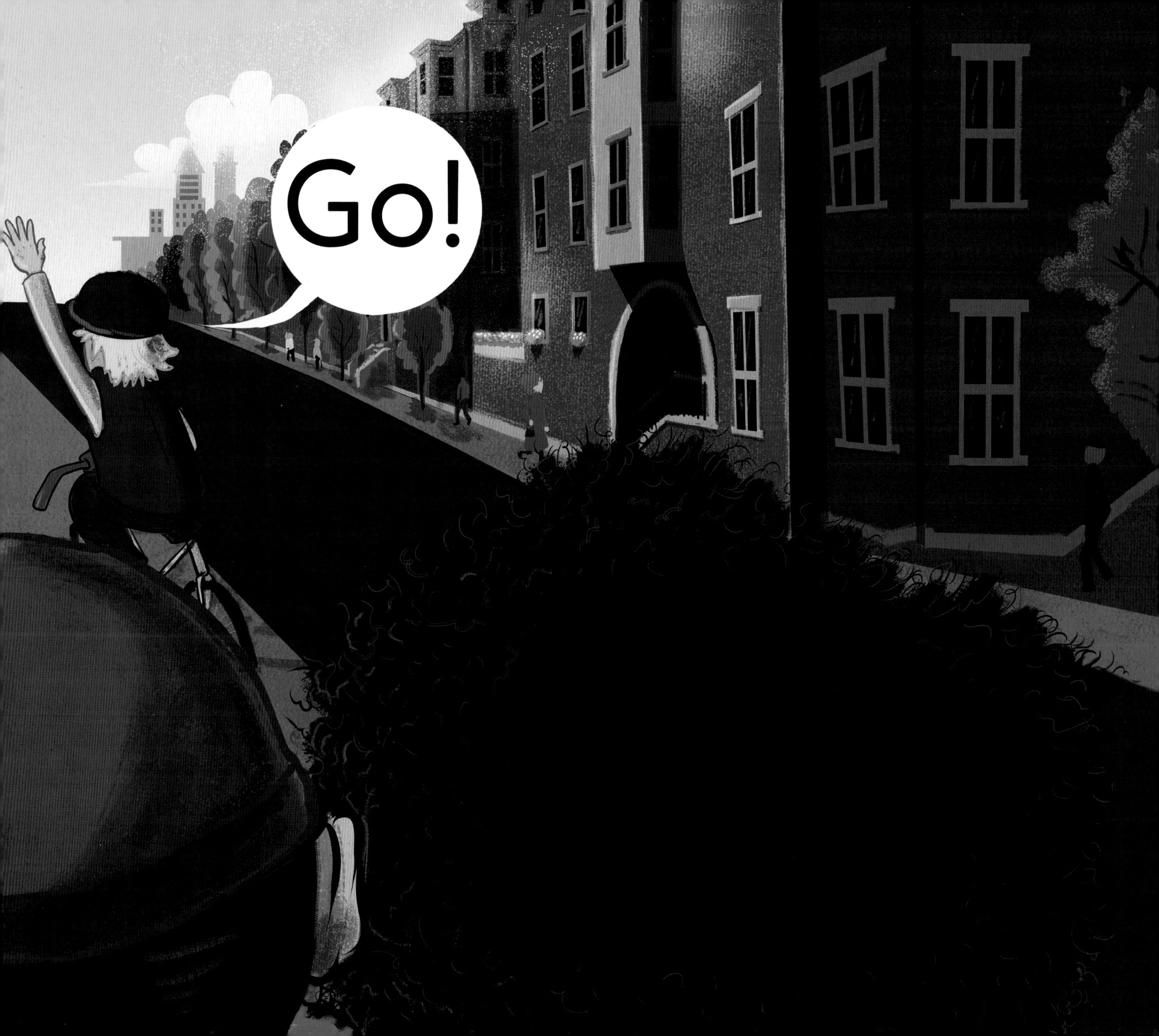
Go!

Bessie zoomed
past the boys.

She sailed over the concrete like it was the ocean in her dream. She was fast enough.

Bessie rode between the old ladies with their yappy dogs like they were the tall buildings in her dream.

Bessie rode out in front as fast as a comet.
She was more than fast enough.

Bessie stopped at the end of the road
and waited for the boys to catch up.

When they caught up, they took turns
clapping hands and giving her pats on the back.

Bessie, you
sure are fast
enough!

Bessie knew now that she really was fast enough!

Bye,
Bessie!

Bessie
is fast!

From then on, Bessie always rode fast, whooshing and speeding every chance she could.

Then one day, she heard a loud noise.

VAAROOM!

Bessie realized she could
be even faster.

Wow, now
that's fast!

About Bessie Stringfield...

Bessie Stringfield became an incredible pioneer for women in motorcycling. She rode fast and traveled to many places that were dangerous for black people in the early and mid-twentieth century. Also, this was during a time when many people thought that it was improper for women to ride motorcycles at all.

Bessie often used *The Negro Motorist Green Book* on her adventures. This was a guidebook by Victor Hugo Green that listed hotels where it was safe for black people traveling in America to stay for the night without other people causing them trouble. It listed where it was safe to stop for gas on the road, to eat, and even to go to the bathroom! During her adventures, Bessie sometimes had to hide in the woods and sleep on her bike because the nearest hotel would not serve black people.

Bessie continued to ride all her life. Bessie did not just ride a motorcycle—she was an adventurer! Bessie called her adventures "Penny Tours." She would toss a penny at a map. Then, wherever it landed she would ride there, just because she could. If she ran out of money along the way, she would earn some by joining a local circus or carnival and performing motorcycle stunts as the "Negro Motorcycle Queen."

During her life, Bessie had many achievements. She earned a nursing degree. She was the only woman on a team of civilian motorcycle couriers for the U.S. military. She rode all over the United States and all over the world. She became one of the first women to ride a motorcycle across America. She made that trek eight times during the 1930s and '40s.

This book is the sort of story that Bessie loved to tell. Bessie was a great teller of tales. Sometimes they were small, sometimes they were big. On her travels she met many people, and she often told stories about her adventures with them.

One of the stories about her own childhood that Bessie repeated often was that she was born in Jamaica in 1911 and came to America as a child with her white mother and black father. Soon after they arrived, said Bessie, her mother died. Her father sent her to an orphanage in Boston, Massachusetts.

She was raised by kindly nuns who taught her a strong sense of religion. Then she was adopted by an Irish Catholic woman who gave her anything she wanted if she prayed for it and "asked the Man Upstairs." This included her first motorcycle at age sixteen, and thus began the legend.

However, new information paints a different picture. It reveals that Bessie was born in Edenton, North Carolina, to a black couple. She said in interviews that she did not have any family, but the truth was that she had family members all over the eastern United States. This kind of contradicting information often follows people whose adventures are larger than life. It's usually a slow process for someone's life story to turn into made-up myths and larger-than-life legends.

But one thing is for sure, Bessie's life was never slow. Whether she was Betsy Ellis, from Kingston, Jamaica, or Bessie Beatrice White from North Carolina, Bessie Stringfield was an amazing woman, and that is all that really matters. In an interview, Bessie said about her life: "Man, I was something." The Motorcycle Queen was telling the truth. She *was* something.

ISBN: 978-1-5493-0314-2

Library of Congress Control Number: 2018953988

Fast Enough: Bessie Stringfield's First Ride © 2019 Joel Christian Gill. Published 2019 by The Lion Forge, LLC.
LION FORGE™ and CUBHOUSE™ and all associated distinctive designs are trademarks of The Lion Forge, LLC.
All rights reserved. Printed in China.

10 9 8 7 6 5 4 3 2 1